'Curiosity is the
most fleeting
of pleasures;
the moment it
is satisfied, it
ceases to exist
and it always
proves very,
very expensive'

ANGELA CARTER
Born 7 May 1940, Eastbourne
Died 16 February 1992, London

All stories in this collection first published in Great Britain
in *The Fairy Tales of Charles Perrault*, 1977.

ALSO PUBLISHED BY PENGUIN BOOKS
The Fairy Tales of Charles Perrault · *Heroes and Villains* ·
The Infernal Desire Machines of Doctor Hoffman

ANGELA CARTER

Bluebeard

PENGUIN BOOKS

PENGUIN CLASSICS

Published by the Penguin Group
Penguin Books Ltd, 80 Strand, London WC2R ORL, England
Penguin Group (USA) Inc., 375 Hudson Street, New York, New York 10014, USA
Penguin Group (Canada), 90 Eglinton Avenue East, Suite 700, Toronto, Ontario,
Canada M4P 2Y3 (a division of Pearson Penguin Canada Inc.)
Penguin Ireland, 25 St Stephen's Green, Dublin 2, Ireland
(a division of Penguin Books Ltd)
Penguin Group (Australia), 250 Camberwell Road, Camberwell, Victoria 3124, Australia
(a division of Pearson Australia Group Pty Ltd)
Penguin Books India Pvt Ltd, 11 Community Centre, Panchsheel Park,
New Delhi – 110 017, India
Penguin Group (NZ), 67 Apollo Drive, Rosedale, North Shore 0632, New Zealand
(a division of Pearson New Zealand Ltd)
Penguin Books (South Africa) (Pty) Ltd, 24 Sturdee Avenue, Rosebank, Johannesburg 2196
South Africa
Penguin Books Ltd, Registered Offices: 80 Strand, London WC2R ORL, England

www.penguin.com

Selected from *The Fairy Tales of Charles Perrault*, published in Penguin Classics 2008
This edition published in Penguin Classics 2011

3

Translation and copyright © Angela Carter, 1977

Typeset by Jouve (UK), Milton Keynes
Printed in England by Clays Ltd, St Ives plc

ISBN: 978-0-141-19588-9

www.greenpenguin.co.uk

Penguin Books is committed to a sustainable future
for our business, our readers and our planet.
The book in your hands is made from paper
certified by the Forest Stewardship Council.

Contents

Bluebeard

There once lived a man who owned fine town houses and fine country houses, dinner services of gold and silver, tapestry chairs and gilded coaches; but, alas, God had also given him a blue beard, which made him look so ghastly that women fled at the sight of him.

A certain neighbour of his was the mother of two beautiful daughters. He decided to marry one or other of them, but he left the girls to decide between themselves which of them should become his wife; whoever would take him could have him. But neither of them wanted him; both felt a profound distaste for a man with a blue beard. They were even more suspicious of him because he had been married several times before and nobody knew what had become of his wives.

In order to make friends with the girls, Bluebeard threw a lavish house-party at one of his country mansions for the sisters, their mother, three or four of their closest friends and several neighbours. The party lasted for eight whole days. Every day there were elaborate parties of pleasure – fishing, hunting, dancing, games, feasting. The guests hardly slept at all but spent the night playing practical jokes on one another. Everything went so well that the youngest daughter began to think that the beard of the master of the house was not so very blue, after all; that he was, all in all, a very fine fellow.

As soon as they returned to town, the marriage took place.

After a month had passed, Bluebeard told his wife he must leave her to her own devices for six weeks or so; he had urgent business in the provinces and must attend to it immediately. But he urged her to enjoy herself while he was away; her friends should visit her and, if she wished, she could take them to the country with her. But, above all, she must keep in good spirits.

'Look!' he said to her. 'Here are the keys of my two large attics, where the furniture is stored; this is the key to the cabinet in which I keep the dinner services of gold and silver that are too good to use every day; these are the keys of the strong-boxes in which I keep my money; these are the keys of my chests of precious stones; and this is the pass key that will let you into every one of the rooms in my mansion. Use these keys freely. All is yours. But this little key, here, is the key of the room at the end of the long gallery on the ground floor; open everything, go everywhere, but I absolutely forbid you to go into that little room and, if you so much as open the door, I warn you that nothing will spare you from my wrath.'

She promised to do as he told her. He kissed her, got into his carriage and drove away.

Her friends and neighbours did not wait until she sent for them to visit her. They were all eager to see the splendours of her house. None of them had dared to call while the master was at home because his blue beard was so offensive. But now they could explore all the rooms at leisure and each one was more sumptuous than the last. They climbed into the attics and were lost for words with which to admire the number and beauty of the tapestries, the beds, the sofas, the cabinets, the tables, and the long mirrors, some of which had frames of glass, others of silver or gilded vermilion – all more magnificent than anything they had ever seen. They never stopped congratulating their friend on her good luck, but she took no pleasure from the sight of all this luxury because she was utterly consumed with the desire to open the door of the forbidden room.

Her curiosity so tormented her that, at last, without stopping to think how rude it was to leave her friends, she ran down the little staircase so fast she almost tripped and broke her neck. When she reached the door of the forbidden room, she stopped for a moment and remembered that her husband had absolutely forbidden her to go inside. She wondered if he would punish her for being disobedient; but the temptation was so strong she could not resist it. She took the little key, and, trembling, opened the door.

The windows were shuttered and at first she could see nothing; but, after a few moments, her eyes grew accustomed to the gloom and she saw that the floor was covered with clotted blood. In the blood lay the corpses of all the women whom Bluebeard had married and then murdered, one after the other. She thought she was going to die of fright and the key fell from her hand. After she came to her senses, she picked up the key, closed the door and climbed back to her room to recover herself.

She saw the key of this forbidden room was stained with blood and washed it. But the blood would not go away, so she washed it again. Still the blood-stain stayed. She washed it, yet again, more carefully, then scrubbed it with soap and sandstone; but the blood-stain would not budge. It was a magic key and nothing could clean it. When the blood was scrubbed from one side of the key, the stain immediately reappeared on the other side.

That same night, Bluebeard returned unexpectedly

from his journey; a letter had arrived on the way to tell him that his business had already been satisfactorily settled in his absence. His wife did all she could to show him how delighted she was to have him back with her so quickly.

Next day, he asked for his keys; she gave them to him but her hand was trembling so badly he guessed what had happened.

'How is it that the key of the little room is no longer with the others?' he asked.

'I must have left it upstairs on my dressing-table,' she said, flustered.

'Give it to me,' said Bluebeard.

She made excuse after excuse but there was no way out; she must go and fetch the key. Bluebeard examined it carefully and said to his wife:

'Why is there blood on this key?'

'I don't know,' quavered the poor woman, paler than death.

'You don't know!' said Bluebeard. 'But *I* know, very well! You have opened the door of the forbidden room. Well, madame, now you have opened it, you may step straight inside it and take your place beside the ladies whom you have seen there!'

She threw herself at her husband's feet, weeping and begging his forgiveness; she was truly sorry she had been disobedient. She was so beautiful and so distressed that the sight of her would have melted a heart of stone, but Bluebeard's heart was harder than any stone.

'You must die, madame,' he said. 'And you must die quickly.'

She looked at him with eyes full of tears and pleaded:

'Since I must die, give me a little time to pray.'

Bluebeard said: 'I'll give you a quarter of an hour, but not one moment more.'

As soon as she was alone, she called to her sister, Anne, and said:

'Sister Anne, climb to the top of the tower and see if my brothers are coming; they told me they would come to visit me today and if you see them, signal to them to hurry.'

Sister Anne climbed to the top of the tower and the poor girl called out to her every minute or so:

'Sister Anne, Sister Anne, do you see anybody coming?'

And Anne, her sister, would reply:

'I see nothing but the sun shining and the grass growing green.'

Bluebeard took an enormous cutlass in his hand and shouted to his wife: 'Come down at once, or I'll climb up to you!'

'Oh, please, I beg you – just a moment more!' she

implored, and called out, in a lower voice: 'Sister Anne, Sister Anne, do you see anybody coming?'

Sister Anne replied:

'I see nothing but the sun shining and the grass growing green.'

'Come down at once, or I'll climb up to you!' cried Bluebeard.

'I'll be down directly,' his wife assured him; but still she whispered: 'Sister Anne, Sister Anne, do you see anything coming?'

'I see a great cloud of dust drawing near from the edge of the horizon.'

'Is it the dust my brothers make as they ride towards me?'

'Oh, no – it is the dust raised by a flock of sheep!'

'Will you never come down?' thundered Bluebeard.

'Just one moment more!' begged his wife and once again she demanded: 'Sister Anne, Sister Anne, do you see anything coming?'

'I see two horsemen in the distance, still far away. Thank God!' she cried a moment later. 'They are our brothers; I shall signal to them to hurry.'

Bluebeard now shouted so loudly that all the house trembled. His unfortunate wife went down to him and threw herself in tears at his feet, her dishevelled hair tumbling around her.

'Nothing you can do will save you,' said Bluebeard. 'You must die.' With one hand, he seized her disordered hair and, with the other, raised his cutlass in the air; he meant to chop off her head with it. The poor woman turned her terrified eyes upon him and begged him for a last moment in which to prepare for death.

'No, no!' he said. 'Think of your maker.' And so he lifted up his cutlass. At that moment came such a loud banging on the door that Bluebeard stopped short. The door opened and in rushed two horsemen with naked blades in their hands.

He recognized his wife's two brothers; one was a dragoon, the other a musketeer. He fled, to save himself, but the two brothers trapped him before he reached the staircase. They thrust their swords through him and left him for dead. Bluebeard's wife was almost as overcome as her husband and did not have enough strength left to get to her feet and kiss her brothers.

Bluebeard left no heirs, so his wife took possession of all his estate. She used part of it to marry her sister, Anne, to a young man with whom she had been in love for a long time; she used more of it to buy commissions for her two brothers; and she used the rest to marry herself to an honest man who made her forget her sorrows as the wife of Bluebeard.

Moral

Curiosity is a charming passion but may only be satisfied at the price of a thousand regrets; one sees around one a thousand examples of this sad truth every day. Curiosity is the most fleeting of pleasures; the moment it is satisfied, it ceases to exist and it always proves very, very expensive.

Another Moral

It is easy to see that the events described in this story took place many years ago. No modern husband would dare to be half so terrible, nor to demand of his wife such an impossible thing as to stifle her curiosity. Be he never so quarrelsome or jealous, he'll toe the line as soon as she tells him to. And whatever colour his beard might be, it's easy to see which of the two is the master.

Little Red Riding Hood

Once upon a time, deep in the heart of the country, there lived a pretty little girl whose mother adored her, and her grandmother adored her even more. This good woman made her a red hood like the ones that fine ladies wear when they go riding. The hood suited the child so much that soon everybody was calling her Little Red Riding Hood.

One day, her mother baked some cakes on the griddle and said to Little Red Riding Hood:

'Your granny is sick; you must go and visit her. Take her one of these cakes and a little pot of butter.'

Little Red Riding Hood went off to the next village to visit her grandmother. As she walked through the wood, she met a wolf, who wanted to eat her but did not dare to because there were woodcutters working nearby. He asked her where she was going. The poor child did not know how dangerous it is to chatter away to wolves and replied innocently:

'I'm going to visit my grandmother to take her this cake and this little pot of butter from my mother.'

'Does your grandmother live far away?' asked the wolf.

'Oh, yes,' said Little Red Riding Hood. 'She lives beyond the mill you can see over there, in the first house you come to in the village.'

'Well, I shall go and visit her, too,' said the wolf. 'I will take *this* road and you shall take *that* road and let's see who can get there first.'

The wolf ran off by the shortest path and Red Riding Hood went off the longest way and she made it still longer because she dawdled along, gathering nuts and chasing butterflies and picking bunches of wayside flowers.

The wolf soon arrived at Grandmother's house. He knocked on the door, rat tat tat.

'Who's there?'

'Your grand-daughter, Little Red Riding Hood,' said the wolf, disguising his voice. 'I've brought you a cake baked on the griddle and a little pot of butter from my mother.'

Grandmother was lying in bed because she was poorly. She called out:

'Lift up the latch and walk in!'

The wolf lifted the latch and opened the door. He

had not eaten for three days. He threw himself on the good woman and gobbled her up. Then he closed the door behind him and lay down in Grandmother's bed to wait for Little Red Riding Hood. At last she came knocking on the door, rat tat tat.

'Who's there?'

Little Red Riding Hood heard the hoarse voice of the wolf and thought that her grandmother must have caught a cold. She answered:

'It's your grand-daughter, Little Red Riding Hood. I've brought you a cake baked on the griddle and a little pot of butter from my mother.'

The wolf disguised his voice and said:

'Lift up the latch and walk in.'

Little Red Riding Hood lifted the latch and opened the door.

When the wolf saw her come in, he hid himself under the bedclothes and said to her:

'Put the cake and the butter down on the bread-bin and come and lie down with me.'

Little Red Riding Hood took off her clothes and went to lie down in the bed. She was surprised to see how odd her grandmother looked. She said to her:

'Grandmother, what big arms you have!'

'All the better to hold you with, my dear.'

'Grandmother, what big legs you have!'

'All the better to run with, my dear.'
'Grandmother, what big ears you have!'
'All the better to hear with, my dear.'
'Grandmother, what big eyes you have!'
'All the better to see with, my dear!'
'Grandmother, what big teeth you have!'
'All the better to eat you up!'

At that, the wicked wolf threw himself upon Little Red Riding Hood and gobbled her up, too.

Moral

Children, especially pretty, nicely brought-up young ladies, ought never to talk to strangers; if they are foolish enough to do so, they should not be surprised if some greedy wolf consumes them, elegant red riding hoods and all.

Now, there are real wolves, with hairy pelts and enormous teeth; but also wolves who seem perfectly charming, sweet-natured and obliging, who pursue young girls in the street and pay them the most flattering attentions.

Unfortunately, these smooth-tongued, smooth-pelted wolves are the most dangerous beasts of all.

Puss in Boots

A certain poor miller had only his mill, his ass and his cat to bequeath to his three sons when he died. The children shared out their patrimony and did not bother to call in the lawyers; if they had done so, they would have been stripped quite bare, of course. The eldest took the mill, the second the ass and the youngest had to make do with the cat.

He felt himself very ill used.

'My brothers can earn an honest living with their inheritance, but once I've eaten my cat and made a muff with his pelt, I shall have to die of hunger.'

The cat overheard him but decided to pretend he had not done so; he addressed his master gravely.

'Master, don't fret; give me a bag and a pair of boots to protect my little feet from the thorny undergrowth and you'll see that your father hasn't provided for you so badly, after all.'

Although the cat's master could not really believe his cat would support him, he had seen him play so many cunning tricks when he went to catch rats and mice – he would hang upside down by his feet; or hide himself in the meal and play at being dead – that he felt a faint hope his cat might think up some helpful scheme.

When the cat had got what he asked for, he put on his handsome boots and slung the bag round his neck, keeping hold of the draw-strings with his two front paws. He went to a warren where he knew there were a great many rabbits. He put some bran and a selection of juicy weeds at the bottom of the bag and then stretched out quite still, like a corpse, and waited for some ingenuous young rabbit to come and investigate the bag and its appetizing contents.

No sooner had he lain down than a silly bunny jumped into the bag. Instantly, the cat pulled the draw-strings tight and killed the rabbit without mercy.

Proudly bearing his prey, he went to the king and asked to speak to him. He was taken to his majesty's private apartment. As soon as he got inside the door, he made the king a tremendous bow and said:

'Sire, may I present you with a delicious young rabbit that my master, the Marquis of Carabas, ordered me to offer to you, with his humblest compliments.'

Without his master's knowledge or consent, the cat had decided the miller's son should adopt the name of the Marquis of Carabas.

'Tell your master that I thank him with all my heart,' said the king.

The next day, the cat hid himself in a cornfield, with his open bag, and two partridges flew into it. He pulled the strings and caught them both. Then he went to present them to the king, just as he had done with the rabbit. The king accepted the partridges with great glee and rewarded the cat with a handsome tip.

The cat kept on taking his master's game to the king for two or three months. One day, he learned that the king planned to take a drive along the riverside with his beautiful daughter. He said to his master:

'If you take my advice, your fortune is made. You just go for a swim in the river at a spot I'll show to you and leave the rest to me.'

The Marquis of Carabas obediently went off to swim, although he could not think why the cat should want him to. While he was bathing, the king drove by and the cat cried out with all its might:

'Help! Help! The Marquis of Carabas is drowning!'

The king put his head out of his carriage window when he heard this commotion and recognized the cat who had brought him so much game. He ordered his servants to hurry and save the Marquis of Carabas.

While they were pulling the marquis out of the river, the cat went to the king's carriage and told him how robbers had stolen his master's clothes while he swam in the river even though he'd shouted 'Stop thief!' at the top of his voice. In fact, the cunning cat had hidden the miller's son's wretched clothes under a stone.

The king ordered the master of his wardrobe to hurry back to the palace and bring a selection of his own finest garments for the Marquis of Carabas to wear. When the young man put them on, he looked very handsome and the king's daughter thought: 'What an attractive young man!' The Marquis of Carabas treated her with respect mingled with tenderness and she fell madly in love.

The king invited the Marquis of Carabas to join him in his carriage and continue the drive in style. The cat was delighted to see his scheme begin to succeed and busily ran ahead of the procession. He came to a band of peasants who were mowing a meadow and said:

'Good people, if you don't tell the king that this meadow belongs to the Marquis of Carabas, I'll make mincemeat of every one of you.'

As soon as he saw the mowers, the king asked them

who owned the hayfield. They had been so intimidated by the cat that they dutifully chorused:

'It belongs to the Marquis of Carabas.'

'You have a fine estate,' remarked the king to the marquis.

'The field crops abundantly every year,' improvised the marquis.

The cat was still racing ahead of the party and came to a band of harvesters. He said to them:

'Good harvesters, if you don't say that all these corn-fields belong to the Marquis of Carabas, I'll make mincemeat of every one of you.'

The king passed by a little later and wanted to know who owned the rolling cornfield.

'The Marquis of Carabas possesses them all,' said the harvesters.

The king expressed his increasing admiration of the marquis's estates. The cat ran before the carriage and made the same threats to everyone he met on the way; the king was perfectly astonished at the young man's great possessions.

At last the cat arrived at a castle. In this castle, lived an ogre. This ogre was extraordinarily rich; he was the true owner of all the land through which the king had travelled. The cat had taken good care to find out all he could about this ogre and now he asked the servant who answered the door if he could speak to him; he said he couldn't pass so close by the castle without paying his respects to such an important man as its owner.

The ogre made him as welcome as an ogre can.

'I'm told you can transform yourself into all sorts of animals,' said the cat. 'That you can change yourself into a lion, for example; or even an elephant.'

'Quite right,' replied the ogre. 'Just to show you, I'll turn myself into a lion.'

When he found himself face to face with a lion, even our cat was so scared that he jumped up on to the roof and balanced there precariously because his boots weren't made for walking on tiles.

As soon as the ogre had become himself again, the cat clambered down and confessed how terrified he had been.

'But gossip also has it – though I can scarcely believe it – that you also have the power to take the shapes of the very smallest animals. They say you can even shrink down as small as a rat, or a mouse. But I must admit, even if it seems rude, that I think that's quite impossible.'

'Impossible?' said the ogre. 'Just you see!' He changed into a mouse and began to scamper around on the floor. The cat no sooner saw him than he jumped on him and gobbled him up.

Meanwhile, the king saw the ogre's fine castle as he drove by and decided to pay it a visit. The cat heard the sound of carriage wheels on the drawbridge, ran outside and greeted the king.

'Welcome, your majesty, to the castle of the Marquis of Carabas.'

'What, sir? Does this fine castle also belong to you? I've never seen anything more splendid than this courtyard and the battlements that surround it; may we be permitted to view the interior?'

The marquis gave his hand to the young princess and followed the king. They entered a grand room where they found a banquet ready prepared; the ogre had invited all his friends to a dinner party, but none of the guests dared enter the castle when they saw the king had arrived. The king was delighted with the good qualities of the Marquis of Carabas and his daughter was beside herself about them. There was also the young man's immense wealth to be taken into account. After his fifth or sixth glass of wine, the king said:

'Say the word, my fine fellow, and you shall become my son-in-law.'

The marquis bowed very low, immediately accepted the honour the king bestowed on him and married the princess that very day. The cat was made a great lord and gave up hunting mice, except for pleasure.

Moral

A great inheritance may be a fine thing; but hard work and ingenuity will take a young man further than his father's money.

Another Moral

If a miller's son can so quickly win the heart of a princess, that is because clothes, bearing and youth speedily inspire affection; and the means to achieve them are not always entirely commendable.

The Sleeping Beauty in the Wood

Once upon a time, there lived a king and a queen who were bitterly unhappy because they did not have any children. They visited all the clinics, all the specialists, made holy vows, went on pilgrimages and said their prayers regularly but with so little success that when, at long last, the queen finally *did* conceive and, in due course, gave birth to a daughter, they were both wild with joy. Obviously, this baby's christening must be the grandest of all possible christenings; for her godmothers, she would have as many fairies as they could find in the entire kingdom. According to the custom of those times, each fairy would make the child a magic present, so that the princess could acquire every possible perfection. After a long search, they managed to trace seven suitable fairies.

After the ceremony at the church, the guests went back to the royal palace for a party in honour of the fairy godmothers. Each of these important guests found her place was specially laid with a great dish of gold and a golden knife, fork and spoon studded with diamonds and rubies. But as the fairies took their seats, an uninvited guest came storming into the palace, deeply affronted because she had been forgotten – though it was no wonder she'd been overlooked; this old fairy had hidden herself away in her tower for fifteen years and, since nobody had set eyes on her all that time, they thought she was dead, or had been bewitched. The king ordered a place to be laid for her at once but he could not give her a great gold dish and gold cutlery like the other fairies had because only seven sets had been made. The old fairy was very annoyed at that and muttered threats between her teeth. The fairy who sat beside her overheard her and suspected she planned to revenge herself by giving the little princess a very unpleasant present when the time for present giving came. She slipped away behind the tapestry so that she could have the last word, if necessary, and put right any harm the old witch might do the baby.

Now the fairies presented their gifts. The first fairy said the princess would grow up to be the loveliest woman in the world. The next said she would have the disposition of an angel, the third that she would be graceful as a gazelle, the fourth gave her the gift of dancing, the fifth of singing like a nightingale, and the

24

sixth said she would be able to play any kind of musical instrument that she wanted to.

But when it came to the old fairy's turn, she shook with spite and announced that, in spite of her beauty and accomplishments, the princess was going to prick her finger with a spindle and die of it.

All the guests trembled and wept. But the youngest fairy stepped out from behind the tapestry and cried out:

'Don't despair, King and Queen; your daughter will not die – though, alas, I cannot undo entirely the magic of a senior-ranking fairy. The princess *will* prick her finger with a spindle but, instead of dying, she will fall into a deep sleep that will last for a hundred years. And at the end of a hundred years, the son of a king will come to wake her.'

In spite of this comfort, the king did all he could to escape the curse; he forbade the use of a spindle, or even the possession of one, on pain of death, in all the lands he governed.

Fifteen or sixteen years went by. The king and queen were spending the summer at a castle in the country and one day the princess decided to explore, prowling through room after room until at last she climbed up a spiral staircase in a tower and came to an attic in which an old lady was sitting, along with her distaff, spinning, for this old lady had not heard how the king had banned the use of a spindle.

'Whatever are you doing, my good woman?' asked the princess.

'I'm spinning, my pretty dear,' answered the old lady.

'Oh, how clever!' said the princess. 'How do you do it? Give it to me so that I can see if I can do it, too!'

She was very lively and just a little careless; but besides, and most importantly, the fairies had ordained it. No sooner had she picked up the spindle than she pierced her hand with it and fell down in a faint.

The old lady cried for help and the servants came running from all directions. They threw water over her, unlaced her corsets, slapped her hands, rubbed her temples with eau-de-cologne – but nothing would wake her.

The king climbed to the attic to see the cause of the clamour and, sad at heart, knew the fairy's curse had come true. He knew the princess's time had come, just as the fairies said it would, and ordered her to be carried to the finest room in the palace and laid there on a bed covered with gold and silver embroidery. She was as beautiful as an angel. Her trance had not yet taken the colour from her face; her cheeks were rosy and her lips like coral. Her eyes were closed but you could hear her breathing very, very softly and, if you saw the slow movement of her breast, you knew she was not dead.

The king ordered she should be left in peace until the time came when she would wake up. At the moment the princess had pricked her finger, the good fairy who saved her life was in the realm of Mataquin, twelve thousand leagues away, but she heard the news immediately from a dwarf who sped to her in a pair of seven-league boots. The fairy left Mataquin at once in a fiery chariot drawn by dragons and arrived at the grieving court an hour later. The king went out to help her down; she approved of all his arrangements but she was very sensitive, and she thought how sad the princess would be when she woke up all alone in that great castle.

So she touched everything in the house, except for the king and queen, with her magic ring – the housekeepers, the maids of honour, the chambermaids, the gentlemen-in-waiting, the court officials, the cooks, the scullions, the errand-boys, the night-watchmen, the Swiss guards, the page-boys, the footmen; she touched all the horses in the stable, and the stable-boys, too, and even Puff, the princess's little lap-dog, who was curled up on her bed beside her. As soon as she touched them with her magic ring, they all fell fast asleep and would not wake up until their mistress woke, ready to look after her when she needed them. Even the spits on the fire, loaded with partridges and pheasants, drowsed off to sleep, and the flames died down and slept, too. All this took only a moment; fairies are fast workers.

The king and queen kissed their darling child but she did not stir. Then they left the palace for ever and issued proclamations forbidding anyone to approach it. Within a quarter of an hour, a great number of trees, some large, some small, interlaced with brambles and thorns, sprang up around the park and formed a hedge so thick that neither man nor beast could penetrate it. This hedge grew so tall that you could see only the topmost turrets of the castle, for the fairy had made a safe, magic place where the princess could sleep her sleep out free from prying eyes.

At the end of a hundred years, the son of the king who now ruled over the country went out hunting in that region. He asked the local police what those turrets he could see above the great wood might mean. They replied, each one, as he had heard tell – how it was an old ruin, full of ghosts; or, that all the witches of the country went there to hold their sabbaths. But the most popular story was that it was the home of an ogre who carried all the children he caught there, to eat them at his leisure, knowing nobody else could follow him through the wood.

The prince did not know what to believe. Then an old man said to him:

'My lord, fifty years ago I heard my father say that the most beautiful princess in all the world was sleeping in that castle, and her sleep was going to last for a hundred years, until the prince who is meant to have her comes to wake her up.'

When he heard that, the young prince was tremendously excited; he had never heard of such a marvellous adventure and, fired with thoughts of love and glory, he made up his mind there and then to go through the wood. No sooner had he stepped among the trees than the great trunks and branches, the thorns and brambles parted, to let him pass. He saw the castle at the end of a great avenue and walked towards it, though he was surprised to see that none of his attendants could follow him because the trees sprang together again as soon as he had gone between them. But he did not abandon his quest. A young prince in love is always brave. Then he arrived at a courtyard that seemed like a place where only fear lived.

An awful silence filled it and the look of death was on everything. Man and beast stretched on the ground, like corpses; but the pimples on the red noses of the Swiss guards soon showed him they were not dead at all, but sleeping, and the glasses beside them, with the dregs of wine still at the bottoms, showed how they had dozed off after a spree.

He went through a marble courtyard; he climbed a

staircase; he went into a guardroom, where the guards were lined up in two ranks, each with a gun on his shoulder, and snoring with all their might. He found several rooms full of gentlemen-in-waiting and fine ladies; some stood, some sat, all slept. At last he arrived in a room that was entirely covered in gilding and, there on a bed with the curtains drawn back so that he could see her clearly, lay a princess about fifteen or sixteen years old and she was so lovely that she seemed, almost, to shine. The prince approached her trembling, and fell on his knees before her.

The enchantment was over; the princess woke. She gazed at him so tenderly you would not have thought it was the first time she had ever seen him.

'Is it you, my prince?' she said. 'You have kept me waiting for a long time.'

The prince was beside himself with joy when he heard that and the tenderness in her voice overwhelmed him so that he hardly knew how to reply. He told her he loved her better than he loved himself and though he stumbled over the words, that made her very happy, because he showed so much feeling. He was more tongue-tied than she, because she had had plenty of time to dream of what she would say to him; her good fairy had made sure she had sweet dreams during her long sleep. They talked for hours and still had not said half the things they wanted to say to one another.

But the entire palace had woken up with the princess and everyone was going about his business again. Since none of them were in love, they were all dying of hunger. The chief lady-in-waiting, just as ravenous as the rest, lost patience after a while and told the princess loud and clear that dinner was ready. The prince helped the princess up from the bed and she dressed herself with the greatest magnificence; but when she put on her ruff, the prince remembered how his grandmother had worn one just like it. All the princess's clothes were a hundred years out of fashion, but she was no less beautiful because of that.

Supper was served in the hall of mirrors, while the court orchestra played old tunes on violins and oboes they had not touched for a hundred years. After supper, the chaplain married them in the castle chapel and the chief lady-in-waiting drew the curtains round their bed for them. They did not sleep much, that night; the princess did not feel in the least drowsy. The prince left her in the morning, to return to his father's palace.

The king was anxious because his son had been away so long. The prince told him that he had lost himself in the forest while he was out hunting and had spent the night in a charcoal burner's hut, where his host had given him black bread and cheese to eat. The king believed the story but the queen, the prince's mother, was not so easily hoodwinked when she saw that now the young man spent most of his time out hunting in the forest. Though he always arrived back with an excellent excuse when he had spent two or three nights away from home, his mother soon guessed he was in love.

He lived with the princess for more than two years and he gave her two children. They named the eldest, a daughter, Dawn, because she was so beautiful but they called their little son Day, because he came after Dawn and was even more beautiful still.

The queen tried to persuade her son to tell her his secret but he dared not confide in her. Although he loved her, he feared her, because she came from a family of ogres and his father had married her only because she was very, very rich. The court whispered that the queen still had ogrish tastes and could hardly keep her hands off little children, so the prince thought it best to say nothing about his own babies.

But when the king died and the prince himself became king, he felt confident enough to publicly announce his marriage and install the new queen, his wife, in his royal palace with a great deal of ceremony. And soon after that, the new king decided to declare war on his neighbour, the Emperor Cantalabutte.

He left the governing of his kingdom in his mother's hands and he trusted her to look after his wife and children for him, too, because he would be away at war for the whole summer.

As soon as he was gone, the queen mother sent her daughter-in-law and her grandchildren away to the country, to a house deep in the woods, so that she could satisfy her hideous appetites with the greatest of ease. She herself arrived at the house a few days later and said to the butler:

'I want to eat little Dawn for my dinner tomorrow.'

'Oh, my lady!' exclaimed the butler.

'She's just the very thing I fancy,' said the queen mother in the voice of an ogress famished for fresh meat. 'And I want you to serve her up with sauce Robert.'

The poor man saw he could not argue with a hungry ogress, picked up a carving knife and went to little Dawn's room. She was just four years old. When she saw her dear friend, the butler, she ran up to him, laughing, threw her arms around his neck and asked him where her sweeties were. He burst into tears and the knife fell from his hands. He went down to the farmyard and slaughtered a little lamb instead. He served the lamb up in such a delicious sauce the queen mother said she had never eaten so well in her life and he spirited little Dawn away from harm; he handed her over to his wife, who hid her in a cellar, in the servants' quarters.

Eight days passed. Then the ogress said to the butler:

'I want to eat little Day for my supper.'

The butler was determined to outwit her again. He found little Day playing at fencing with his pet monkey; the child was only three. He took him to his wife, who hid him away with his sister, and served up a tender young kid in his place. The queen mother smacked her lips over the dish, so all went well until the night the wicked ogress said to the butler:

'I want to eat the queen with the same sauce you made for her children.'

This time, the poor butler did not know what to do. The queen was twenty, now, if you did not count the hundred years she had been asleep; her skin was white and lovely but it was a little tough, and where in all the farmyard was he to find a beast with skin just like it? There was nothing for it; he must kill the queen to save himself and he went to her room, determined he would not have to enter it a second time. He rushed in with a dagger in his hand and told her her mother-in-law had ordered her to die.

'Be quick about it,' she said calmly. 'Do as she told you. When I am dead, I shall be with my poor children again, my children whom I love so much.'

Because they had been taken away from her without a word of explanation, she thought they were dead.

The butler's heart melted.

'No, no, my lady, you don't need to die so that you can be with your children. I've hidden them away from the queen mother's hunger and I will trick her again, I will give her a young deer for supper instead of you.'

He took her to the cellar, where he left her kissing her children and weeping over them, and went to kill a young doe that the queen mother ate for supper with as much relish as if it had been her daughter-in-law. She was very pleased with her own cruelty and practised telling her son how the wolves had eaten his wife and children while he had been away at the wars.

One night as she prowled about as usual, sniffing for the spoor of fresh meat, she heard a voice coming from the servants' quarters. It was little Day's voice; he was crying because he had been naughty and his mother wanted to whip him. Then the queen mother heard Dawn begging her mother to forgive the little boy. The ogress recognized the voices of her grandchildren and she was furious. She ordered a huge vat to be brought into the middle of the courtyard. She had the vat filled with toads, vipers, snakes and serpents and then the queen, her children, the butler, his wife and his maid were brought in front of her with their hands tied behind their backs. She was going to have them thrown into the vat.

The executioners were just on the point of carrying out their dreadful instructions when the king galloped into the courtyard. Nobody had expected him back so soon. He was astonished at what he saw and asked who had commanded the vat and the bonds. The ogress was so angry to see her plans go awry that she jumped head-first into the vat and the vile beasts inside devoured her in an instant. The king could not help grieving a little; after all, she was his mother. But his beautiful wife and children soon made him happy again.

Moral

A brave, rich, handsome husband is a prize well worth waiting for; but no modern woman would think it was worth waiting for a hundred years. The tale of the Sleeping Beauty shows how long engagements make for happy marriages, but young girls these days want so much to be married I do not have the heart to press the moral.

Cinderella: or, The Little Glass Slipper

There once lived a man who married twice, and his second wife was the haughtiest and most stuck-up woman in the world. She already had two daughters of her own and her children took after her in every way. Her new husband's first wife had given him a daughter of his own before she died, but she was a lovely and sweet-natured girl, very like her own natural mother, who had been a kind and gentle woman.

The second wedding was hardly over before the step-mother showed her true colours. Her new daughter was so lovable that she made her own children seem even more unpleasant, by contrast; so she found the girl insufferable. She gave her all the rough work about the house to do, washing the pots and pans, cleaning out Madame's bedroom and those of her step-sisters, too. She slept at the top of the house, in a garret, on a thin, lumpy mattress, while her step-sisters had rooms with fitted carpets, soft beds and mirrors in which they could see themselves from head to foot. The poor girl bore everything patiently and dared not complain to her father because he would have lost his temper with her. His new wife ruled him with a rod of iron.

When the housework was all done, she would tuck herself away in the chimney corner to sit quietly among the cinders, the only place of privacy she could find, and so the family nicknamed her Cinderbritches. But the younger sister, who was less spiteful than the older one, changed her nickname to Cinderella. Yet even in her dirty clothes, Cinderella could not help but be a hundred times more beautiful than her sisters, however magnificently they dressed themselves up.

The king's son decided to hold a ball to which he invited all the aristocracy. Our two young ladies received their invitations, for they were well connected. Busy and happy, they set about choosing the dresses and hair-styles that would suit them best and that made more work for Cinderella, who had to iron her sisters' petti-coats and starch their ruffles. They could talk about nothing except what they were going to wear.

'I shall wear my red velvet with the lace trimming,' said the eldest.

'Well, I shall wear just a simple skirt but put my coat with the golden flowers over it and, of course, there's always my diamond necklace, which is really rather special,' said the youngest.

They sent for a good hairdresser to cut and curl their hair and they bought the best cosmetics. They called Cinderella to ask for her advice, because she had excellent taste. Cinderella helped them to look as pretty as they could and they were very glad of her assistance, although they did not show it.

As she was combing their hair, they said to her:

'Cinderella, dear, wouldn't you like to go to the ball yourself?'

'Oh, don't make fun of me, my ladies, how could I possibly go to the ball!'

'Quite right, too; everyone would laugh themselves silly to see Cinderbritches at a ball.'

Any other girl but Cinderella would have made horrid tangles of their hair after that, out of spite; but she was kind, and resisted the temptation. The step-sisters could not eat for two days, they were so excited. They broke more than a dozen corset-laces because they pulled them in so tightly in order to make themselves look slender, and they were always primping in front of the mirror.

At last the great day arrived. When they went off, Cinderella watched them until they were out of sight and then began to cry. Her godmother saw how she was crying and asked her what the matter was.

'I want ... I want to ...'

But Cinderella was crying so hard she could not get the words out.

Her godmother was a fairy. She said: 'I think you're crying because you want to go to the ball.'

'Yes,' said Cinderella, sighing.

'If you are a good girl, I'll send you there,' said her godmother.

She took her into her own room and said:

'Go into the garden and pick me a pumpkin.'

Cinderella went out to the garden and picked the finest pumpkin she could find. She took it to her godmother, although she could not imagine how a pumpkin was going to help her get to the ball. Her godmother hollowed out the pumpkin until there was nothing left but the shell, struck it with her ring – and instantly the pumpkin changed into a beautiful golden coach.

Then the godmother went to look in the mousetrap, and found six live mice there. She told Cinderella to lift up the lid of the trap enough to let the mice come out one by one and, as each mouse crept out, she struck it lightly with her ring. At the touch of the ring, each mouse changed into a carriage horse. Soon the coach had six dappled greys to draw it.

Then she asked herself what would do for a coachman.

'I'll go and see if there is a rat in the rat-trap,' said Cinderella. 'A rat would make a splendid coachman.'

'Yes, indeed,' said her godmother. 'Go and see.'

There were three fat rats in the rat-trap that Cinderella brought to her. One had particularly fine whiskers, so the godmother chose that one; when she struck him with her ring, he changed into a plump coachman who had the most imposing moustache you could wish to see.

'If you look behind the watering-can in the garden, you'll find six lizards,' the godmother told Cinderella. 'Bring them to me.'

No sooner had Cinderella brought them to her godmother than the lizards were all changed into footmen, who stepped up behind the carriage in their laced uniforms and hung on as if they had done nothing else all their lives.

The fairy said to Cinderella:

'There you are! Now you can go to the ball. Aren't you pleased?'

'Yes, of course. But how can I possibly go to the ball in these wretched rags?'

The godmother had only to touch her with her ring

and Cinderella's workaday overalls and apron changed into a dress of cloth of gold and silver, embroidered with precious stones. Then she gave her the prettiest pair of glass slippers. Now Cinderella was ready, she climbed into the coach; but her godmother told her she must be home by midnight because if she stayed at the ball one moment more, her coach would turn back into a pumpkin, her horses to mice, her footmen to lizards and her clothes back into overalls again.

She promised her godmother that she would be sure to return from the ball before midnight. Then she drove off.

The king's son had been told that a great princess, hitherto unknown to anyone present, was about to arrive at the ball and ran to receive her. He himself helped her down from her carriage with his royal hand and led her into the ballroom where all the guests were assembled. As soon as they saw her, an enormous silence descended. The dancing ceased, the fiddlers forgot to ply their bows as the entire company gazed at this unknown lady. The only sound in the entire ballroom was a confused murmur:

'Oh, isn't she beautiful!'

Even the king himself, although he was an old man, could not help gazing at her and remarked to the queen that he had not seen such a lovely young lady for a long time. All the women studied her hair and her ball-gown attentively so that they would be able to copy them the next day, provided they could find such a capable hair-dresser, such a skilful dressmaker, such magnificent silk.

The king's son seated her in the most honoured place and then led her on to the dance floor; she danced so gracefully, she was still more admired. Then there was a fine supper but the prince could not eat at all, he was too preoccupied with the young lady. She herself went and sat beside her sisters and devoted herself to entertaining them. She shared the oranges and lemons the prince had given her with them and that surprised them very much, for they did not recognize her.

While they were talking, Cinderella heard the chimes of the clock striking a quarter to twelve. She made a deep curtsey and then ran off as quickly as she could. As soon as she got home, she went to find her god-mother and thanked her and told her how much she wanted to go to the ball that was to be given the following day, because the king's son had begged her to. While she was telling her godmother everything that had happened, her step-sisters knocked at the door. Cinderella hurried to let them in.

'What a long time you've been!' she said to them

yawning, rubbing her eyes and stretching as if she could scarcely keep awake, although she had not wanted to sleep for a single moment since they had left the house.

'If you had come to the ball, you wouldn't have been sleepy!' said one of the sisters. 'The most beautiful princess you ever saw arrived unexpectedly and she was so kind to us, she gave us oranges and lemons.'

Cinderella asked the name of the princess but they told her nobody knew it, and the king's son was in great distress and would give anything to find out more about her. Cinderella smiled and said:

'Was she really so very beautiful? Goodness me, how lucky you are. And can I never see her for myself? What a shame! Miss Javotte, lend me that old yellow dress you wear around the house so that I can go to the ball tomorrow and see her for myself.'

'What?' exclaimed Javotte. 'Lend my dress to such a grubby little Cinderbritches as it is – it must think I've lost my reason!'

Cinderella had expected a refusal; and she would have been exceedingly embarrassed if her sister had relented and agreed to lend her a dress and taken her to the ball in it.

Next day, the sisters went off to the ball again. Cinderella went, too, but this time she was even more beautifully dressed than the first time. The king's son did not leave her side and never stopped paying her compliments so that the young girl was utterly absorbed in him and time passed so quickly that she thought it must still be only eleven o'clock when she heard the chimes of midnight. She sprang to her feet and darted off as lightly as a doe. The prince sprang after her but could not catch her; in her flight, however, she let fall one of her glass slippers and the prince tenderly picked it up. Cinderella arrived home out of breath, without her carriage, without her footmen, in her dirty old clothes again; nothing remained of all her splendour but one of her little slippers, the pair of the one she had dropped. The prince asked the guards at the palace gate if they had seen a princess go out; they replied they had seen nobody leave the castle last night at midnight but a ragged young girl who looked more like a kitchen-maid than a fine lady.

When her sisters came home from the ball, Cinderella asked them if they had enjoyed themselves again; and had the beautiful princess been there? They said, yes; but she had fled at the very stroke of midnight, and so promptly that she had dropped one of her little glass slippers. The king's son had found it and never took his eyes off it for the rest of the evening, so plainly he was very much in love with the beautiful young lady to whom it belonged.

They spoke the truth. A few days later, the king's son publicly announced that he would marry whoever possessed the foot for which the glass slipper had been made. They made a start by trying the slipper on the feet of all the princesses; then moved on to the duchesses, then to the rest of the court, but all in vain. At last they brought the slipper to the two sisters, who did all they could to squeeze their feet into the slipper but could not manage it, no matter how hard they tried. Cinderella watched them; she recognized her own slipper at once. She laughed, and said:

'I'd like to try and see if it might not fit me!'

Her sisters giggled and made fun of her but the gentleman who was in charge of the slipper trial looked at Cinderella carefully and saw how beautiful she was. Yes, he said; of course she could try on the slipper. He had received orders to try the slipper on the feet of every girl in the kingdom. He sat Cinderella down and, as soon as he saw her foot, he knew it would fit the slipper perfectly. The two sisters were very much astonished but not half so astonished as they were when Cinderella took her own glass slipper from her pocket. At that the godmother appeared; she struck Cinderella's overalls with her ring and at once the old clothes were transformed to garments more magnificent than all her ball-dresses.

Then her sisters knew she had been the beautiful lady they had seen at the ball. They threw themselves at her feet to beg her to forgive them for all the bad treatment she had received from them. Cinderella raised them up and kissed them and said she forgave them with all her heart and wanted them only always to love her. Then, dressed in splendour, she was taken to the prince. He thought she was more beautiful than ever and married her a few days later. Cinderella, who was as good as she was beautiful, took her sisters to live in the palace and arranged for both of them to be married, on the same day, to great lords.

Moral

Beauty is a fine thing in a woman; it will always be admired. But charm is beyond price and worth more, in the long run. When her godmother dressed Cinderella up and told her how to behave at the ball, she instructed her in charm. Lovely ladies, this gift is worth more than a fancy hairdo; to win a heart, to reach a happy ending, charm is the true gift of the fairies. Without it, one can achieve nothing; with it, everything.

Another Moral

It is certainly a great advantage to be intelligent, brave, well-born, sensible and have other similar talents given only by heaven. But however great may be your god-given store, they will never help you to get on in the world unless you have either a godfather or a god-mother to put them to work for you.

Ricky with the Tuft

There was once a queen who gave birth to a son so ugly and ungainly that even his mother's heart could not warm to him at all. But the fairy midwife who attended her told her she would certainly learn to love him because he would grow up to be very clever and exceptionally charming and, she added, because of the gift she was about to make him, he would be able to share his native wit with the one he would love best, when the time came.

So the queen was somewhat consoled for having brought such an ugly object into the world and no sooner had the child learned to speak than he began to chatter away so cleverly, and to behave with so much engaging intelligence, that everyone was charmed by him and he was universally loved. I forgot to tell you that he was born with a little tuft of hair on top of his head, which earned him the nickname: Ricky with the Tuft. Ricky was the name of his family.

At the end of seven or eight years, the queen of a neighbouring country gave birth to twin daughters. The first to be born was as beautiful as the day; the queen was so overjoyed that the nurses were afraid she might lose her senses. The same fairy midwife who had attended the birth of Ricky with the Tuft had arrived to look after this queen, too, and, to calm her excesses, she told her that, alas, the pretty little princess had no sense at all and would grow up to be as stupid as she was beautiful. The queen was very upset to hear that and even more upset, a moment or two later, when her second daughter arrived in the world and *this* one proved to be extraordinarily ugly.

'Don't distress yourself, madame,' said the fairy. 'Your other daughter will have many compensations. She will be so clever and witty that nobody will notice how plain she is.'

'I truly hope so!' exclaimed the queen. 'But isn't there any way we could give this pretty one just a spark or two of the ugly one's wit?'

'I can do nothing for her on that account,' said the fairy. 'But I can certainly make her more beautiful than any girl in the world. And since there is nothing I would not do to make you happy, I am going to give her the power to make whoever it is with whom she falls in love as beautiful as she is, too.'

As the two princesses grew up, their perfections grew
with them and everywhere nobody talked of anything
but the beauty of the elder and the wit and wisdom
of the younger. But age also emphsized their defects.
The younger grew more ugly as you looked at her and
the elder became daily more and more stupid. Either
she was struck dumb the minute somebody spoke to her
or else she said something very foolish in reply. Besides,
she was so clumsy she could not four pots on the
mantelpiece without spilling half on her clothes.

Although beauty is usually a great asset in a young
woman, her younger sister always outshone the
elder in company. First of all, they'd flock around
the lovely one to look at her and as her but soon
she was abandoned for the compan the one with
more to say for herself. And in less t quarter of
hour, there she would be, all by hers the young
the centre of an animated throng. Br e it and she
elder might be, she could not help b out a single
would have sacrificed all her beauty and charm.
regret for half her sister's wit, intell even so, she
The queen tried to prevent herself stupidity now
could not help reproach the girl for want to die
and then and that made the poor pr
for grief.

One day, when she was hiding self in a wood

bemoaning her fate, she saw a little man whose unpre-
possessing appearance was equalled only by the magnificence of his clothes. It was the young prince, Ricky
Tuft, who had fallen head over heels in love
with the pretty pictures of the princess that were on
sale in all the shops. He had left his father's kingdom in
order to see her in the flesh, and speak to her. He was
delighted to meet her accidentally, alone in the wood,
and greeted her with great respect. After he had paid
the usual compliments, he saw how sad she looked

said to her

'Madame, I can't understand how a lady as beautiful
are could possibly be as unhappy as you seem to
have had good fortune to meet a great many
beautiful people but I can truthfully say I've never seen
beautiful as you.'

'You are very kind,' said the princess and, since she
could think of nothing more to say, she fell abruptly
silent.

'Beauty is such a blessing, why! it is more important
than anything,' said Ricky. 'And if one is beautiful, I
don't understand how anything could ever upset one.'

'Oh! I would rather be as ugly as you are and be clever
than be beautiful and as terribly, terribly stupid as me!'

'Nothing reveals true wisdom so much as the conviction one is a fool, madame; and the truly wise are those who know they are fools.'

'I don't know anything about any of that,' said the princess. 'But I do know I really am a fool and that's the reason why I'm so unhappy.'

'If that's the only reason for your unhappiness, madame, then I can cure it in a trice.'

'How can you do that?' asked the princess.

'Well, madame, I have the power to dower the lady whom I love with as much wit as she wishes and, since you are the very one for me, wit and wisdom are yours for the asking if you would consent to become my wife.'

The princess was utterly taken aback and could not speak a single word.

'I see my proposal throws you into a state of confusion,' said Ricky with the Tuft. 'That doesn't surprise me. I will give you a whole year in which to make up your mind.'

The princess had so few brains and such a longing to possess some that she imagined a year would be endless so she accepted his proposal on the spot. No sooner had she promised Ricky with the Tuft that she would marry him that same day in one year's time than she felt a great change come over her. From that moment, she began such a brilliant and witty conversation with Ricky that he thought he must have given her more intelligence than he had kept for himself.

When she went home to the palace, the courtiers did not know what to think of the sudden and extraordinary change in her. Before, she had babbled idiocies; now she said the wisest things, and always with a sweet touch of wit. Everyone was overjoyed, except her younger sister whose nose was put sadly out of joint because, now she no longer outshone her sister in conversation, nothing detracted from her ugliness and she looked the plain little thing she really was beside her.

The king took advice from his counsellors. The news of the change in the princess was publicly announced and all the young princes from the neighbouring kingdoms tried to make her fall in love with them. But she found that not one of them was half as clever as she was and she listened to all their protestations unmoved. However, at last there came a prince so powerful, so rich and so handsome that she felt her interest quicken slightly. Her father told her that she could choose her own husband from among her suitors. She thanked him and asked him for a little time in which to decide.

So that she could make up her mind in peace she went off for a walk by herself and, by chance, she found herself in the same wood where she had met Ricky with the Tuft. As she walked through the wood, deep in thought, she heard a noise under her feet, as if a great many people were coming and going, hither and thither, in a great bustle, underground. Listening attentively, she thought she heard a voice demand: 'Bring me that roasting pan,' and another say: 'Fetch me the saucepan,' and yet another cry: 'Put a bit more wood on the fire.' Then the very ground opened in front of her and she saw a huge kitchen full of cooks, scullions and all the staff required to prepare a magnificent banquet. Out of the kitchen came a band of twenty or thirty spit-turners who at once took up their positions round a long table and, chef's caps on the sides of their heads, larding needles in hand, all went busily to work, singing away.

The princess was astonished at the spectacle and asked them who was their master.

'Why, Prince Ricky with the Tuft, madame,' replied the head cook. 'And tomorrow is his wedding day.'

The princess was more surprised than ever. Then, in a flash, she remembered how, just a year before, she had promised to marry Ricky with the Tuft; and when she remembered that, she thought she would faint. She had forgotten her promise completely. When she had said she would marry Ricky, she had been a fool and, as soon as she possessed all the sense the prince had given her, her earlier follies had vanished from her mind.

In a state of some agitation, she walked on but she

had not gone thirty paces before Ricky with the Tuft presented himself to her, dressed like a prince on his wedding day.

'See, madame!' he said. 'I have come to keep my word and I do not doubt that you are here in order to keep yours.'

'I must confess to you that I have not made up my mind on that point,' answered the princess, 'and I fear that I do not think I shall ever be able to do as you wish.'

'You astonish me, madame,' said Ricky with the Tuft.

'I daresay I do,' said the princess calmly. 'And, certainly, if I were dealing with an insensitive man, I should feel very embarrassed. An insensitive man would say to me: "A princess must keep her word. You promised to marry me and marry me you shall." But I know I am speaking to a subtle and perceptive man of the world and I am certain he will listen to reason. As you know, when I was a fool, I could not bring myself to a firm decision concerning our marriage. Now I have the brains you gave me, I am even more difficult to please than I was then. And would you wish me to make a decision today that I could not make when I had no sense? If you wished to marry me, you did me a great wrong to take away my stupidity and make me see clearly things I never saw before.'

Ricky with the Tuft replied:

'If an insensitive man would be justified in reproaching you for breaking your word, why should you expect, madame, that I should not behave in the same way when my whole life's happiness is at stake? Is it reasonable that a sensitive man should be treated worse than an insensitive one? Would you say that, when you possess so much reason yourself, and wanted it so much? But let us come to the point. With the single exception of my ugliness, is there anything in me that displeases you? Are you dissatisfied with my birth, my intelligence, my personality or my behaviour?'

'Not at all,' replied the princess. 'I love everything about you except your person.'

'If that is so, then I am going to be very happy,' said Ricky with the Tuft. 'For you alone can make me the handsomest of men.'

'How can I do that?' asked the princess.

'By loving me enough to make it come true,' said Ricky. 'The fairy midwife who gave me the power to make the one I loved wise and witty also gave you the power to make the one you love as beautiful as you are yourself, if you truly wish it so.'

'If that is the way of things,' said the princess, 'I wish with all my heart that you may become the handsomest prince in all the world.'

As soon as she said that, Ricky with the Tuft seemed to her the handsomest man she had ever seen.

But some people say there was no magic involved in this transformation and love alone performed the miracle. They whispered that when the princess took into account her lover's faithfulness, his sense, his good qualities, and his intellect, then she no longer saw how warped his body was nor how ugly his face. His hump seemed to her no more than good, broad shoulders; at first she thought he had a frightful limp but now she saw it was really a charming, scholarly stoop. His eyes only sparkled the more because of his squint and she knew that squint was due to the violence of his passion. And how martial, how heroic, she thought his huge, red nose was!

Be that as it may, the princess promised to marry him there and then, provided he obtained consent of the king, her father.

The king saw how much in love his daughter was with Ricky with the Tuft and, besides, he knew him for a wise and prudent prince. He accepted him as his son-in-law with pleasure.

The next day, the wedding was celebrated just as

Ricky had foreseen, according to the arrangements he had made a year before.

Moral

This is not a fairy tale but the plain, unvarnished truth; every feature of the face of the one we love is beautiful, every word the beloved says is wise.

Another Moral

A beautiful soul is one thing, a beautiful face another. But love alone can touch the heart.

The Foolish Wishes

There once lived a woodcutter who was so poor he couldn't enjoy life at all; he thought he was by nature a most unlucky fellow.

One day, at work in the woods, he was moaning away, as usual, when Jupiter, king of the gods, appeared unexpectedly, thunderbolt in hand. The woodcutter was very frightened and threw himself on the ground, apologizing profusely for ever having complained about anything at all.

'Don't be scared,' said Jupiter. 'I'm deeply touched by your misfortunes. Listen. I am the king of the gods and the master of the world. I'm going to grant you three wishes. Anything you want, anything at all, whatever will make you happy – all you have to do is wish for it. But think very carefully before you make your wishes, because they're the only ones you'll ever get.'

At that, Jupiter went noisily back to heaven and the woodcutter picked up his bundle of sticks and trudged home, light at heart. 'I mustn't wish for anything silly,' he said to himself. 'Must talk it all over with the wife before I make a decision.'

When he reached his cottage, he told his wife, Fanchon, to pile more wood on the fire.

'We're going to be rich!' he said. 'All we've got to do is to make three wishes.'

He told her what had happened to him and she was dazzled at the prospects that opened up before her. But she thought they should plan their wishes very carefully.

'Blaise, my dear, don't let's spoil everything by being too hasty. Let's talk things over, and put off making our first wish until tomorrow, after we've had a good night's sleep.'

'Quite right,' said Blaise, her husband. 'But let's celebrate; let's have a glass of wine.'

She drew some wine from the barrel and he rested his bones in his armchair beside a roaring fire, glass in hand, happier than he had ever been in his life.

'My, oh, my,' he said, half to himself. 'I know just what would go down well on a night like this; a nice piece of black pudding. Why, I wish I had a piece of black pudding right now!'

No sooner had he spoken these fateful words than Fanchon beheld an enormous black pudding make an unexpected appearance in the chimney corner and come crawling towards her like a snake. First, she screamed; then, when she realized that the black pudding had arrived solely because her stupid husband had made a careless wish, she called him every name under the sun and heaped abuse on his head.

'We could have had an entire empire of our own! Gold and pearls and diamonds and nice clothes, any amount of them – and what do you go and wish for? What's your heart's desire – why, a bit of black pudding!'

'Well, I'm sorry,' he said. 'What else can I say? I admit it, I've done something very foolish. I'll do better, next time. Haven't I said I'm sorry?'

'Words, words, words,' said the woodcutter's wife. 'Why don't you go and sleep in the stable; it's the best place for an ass like you.'

Her husband lost his temper completely at that and thought how much he'd like to wish to be a widower; but he didn't quite dare say it aloud.

'Men were born to suffer! To hell with the black pudding! I wish that black pudding were hanging from the end of your nose!'

Now, Fanchon was a very pretty woman and nobody would have said her looks were improved by the black pudding but it hung over her mouth and muffled her nagging and, for a single, happy moment, her husband felt he could wish for nothing more.

'After these disasters,' he announced, 'we must be

more prudent. I think I shall use my last remaining wish to make myself a king.'

But, all the same, he had to take the queen's feelings into account; how would she like to be a queen and sit on a throne when she had a nose as long as a donkey's? And, because only one wish was left, that was the choice before them – either King Blaise had for his consort the ugliest queen in the world; or they used the wish to get rid of the pudding and Blaise the woodcutter had his pretty wife again.

Fanchon, however, thought there was no choice at all. She wanted her nose in its original condition. Nothing more.

So the woodcutter stayed in his cottage and went out to saw logs every day. He did not become a king; he did not even fill his pockets with money. He was only too glad to use the last wish to make things as they had been again.

Moral

Greedy, short-sighted, careless, thoughtless, changeable people don't know how to make sensible decisions; and few of us are capable of using well the gifts God gave us, anyway.

a little history

Penguin Modern Classics were launched in 1961, and have been shaping the reading habits of generations ever since.

The list began with distinctive grey spines and evocative pictorial covers – a look that, after various incarnations, continues to influence their current design – and with books that are still considered landmark classics today.

Penguin Modern Classics have caused scandal and political change, inspired great films and broken down barriers, whether social, sexual or the boundaries of language itself. They remain the most provocative, groundbreaking, exciting and revolutionary works of the last 100 years (or so).

In 2011, on the fiftieth anniversary of the Modern Classics, we're publishing fifty Mini Modern Classics: the very best short fiction by writers ranging from Beckett to Conrad, Nabokov to Saki, Updike to Wodehouse. Though they don't take long to read, they'll stay with you long after you turn the final page.

MODERN CLASSICS
www.penguinclassics.com